JOURNEY TO THE
HAUNTED PLANET

Written by A.J.Wood Illustrated by Wayne Anderson

TEMPLAR
PUBLISHING

D1421091

Professor Sponge was going on a day trip to outer space.
"Can we come?" cried Fred and Lucy.
"If you must," said the Professor. "With luck, we might even reach
Pluto before it's time to come home for tea."

They dusted down the Professor's home-made rocket.
Then they put on some special space suits and set off.
Black space and sparkling stars whizzed past
the rocket windows.

Lucy wished that Soap the Dog
was with them - after all,
Star Trek was his favourite
TV show. But the
Professor had said,
"Space is no place for a
dog," and left him at home
to guard the workshop.

Or so they thought...

In fact, Soap had smuggled himself
aboard and was sleeping, wrapped around
a warm pipe.
Trouble was, as soon as he let go,
he started to float around the cabin.

"What are you doing here?" cried the
Professor. "Space is no place for a..."

But before he could finish, something
dreadful happened.
Soap's tail wrapped around a control lever.
There was a terrible lurch.

"Help!" cried the Professor.
"Now we're off course and
heading into deep space.
Drat that dog!"

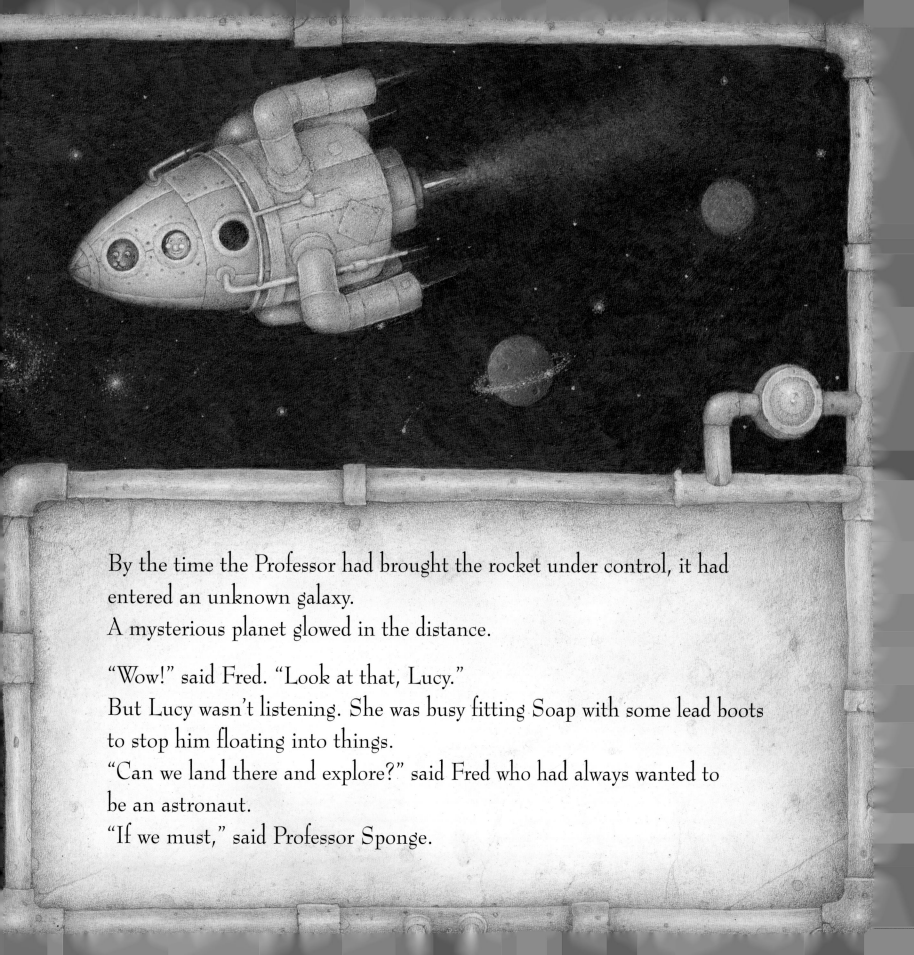

By the time the Professor had brought the rocket under control, it had entered an unknown galaxy.
A mysterious planet glowed in the distance.

"Wow!" said Fred. "Look at that, Lucy."
But Lucy wasn't listening. She was busy fitting Soap with some lead boots to stop him floating into things.
"Can we land there and explore?" said Fred who had always wanted to be an astronaut.
"If we must," said Professor Sponge.

The rocket set down with a thump.
When the spacedust had settled, they put on their helmets (Lucy
had made a special one for Soap) and opened the rocket door.

Out they stepped on to a VERY strange planet indeed!
"I wonder if anyone lives here?" said Lucy.
The Professor checked with a special device on his
belt. "There is no sign of life on this planet,"
he said firmly.

But the Professor was wrong.
Little did he know that they were being watched...

Lucy, Fred and the Professor stepped into a
spooky forest of twisted trees. Strange fossilized creatures
looked down at them from the branches.
"These must be the remains of the creatures that once
lived here," explained the Professor.

Meanwhile, Soap had run on ahead.
He was busy testing out his new boots and thinking about a
career in canine modelling. He was also feeling rather peckish and
thought that somewhere ahead he could smell a juicy bone.

"Come back Soap!" cried Lucy.
Just then there was a loud bark.
Soap had tripped over a tree root and
fallen headfirst down a great
black hole.

"That dog is nothing but trouble," complained the Professor. "We shall have to fetch a rope to rescue him."

But, as he finished speaking, there was a strange rustling noise from amongst the branches.
"Help! ALIENS!!!" cried Lucy.
And, sure enough, there they were, looking very strange indeed.

"Quick! Run for your lives!" cried the Professor and, grabbing Fred and Lucy by the arm, he ran –

straight over the edge of the crater.

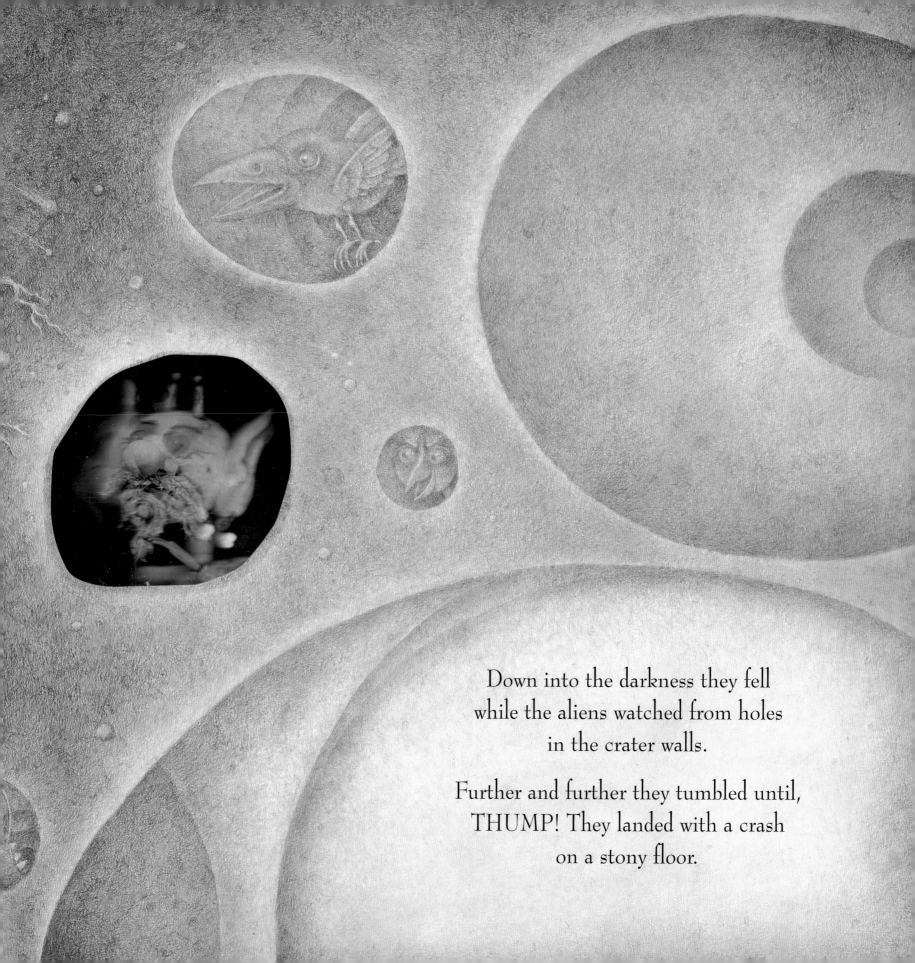

Down into the darkness they fell
while the aliens watched from holes
in the crater walls.

Further and further they tumbled until,
THUMP! They landed with a crash
on a stony floor.

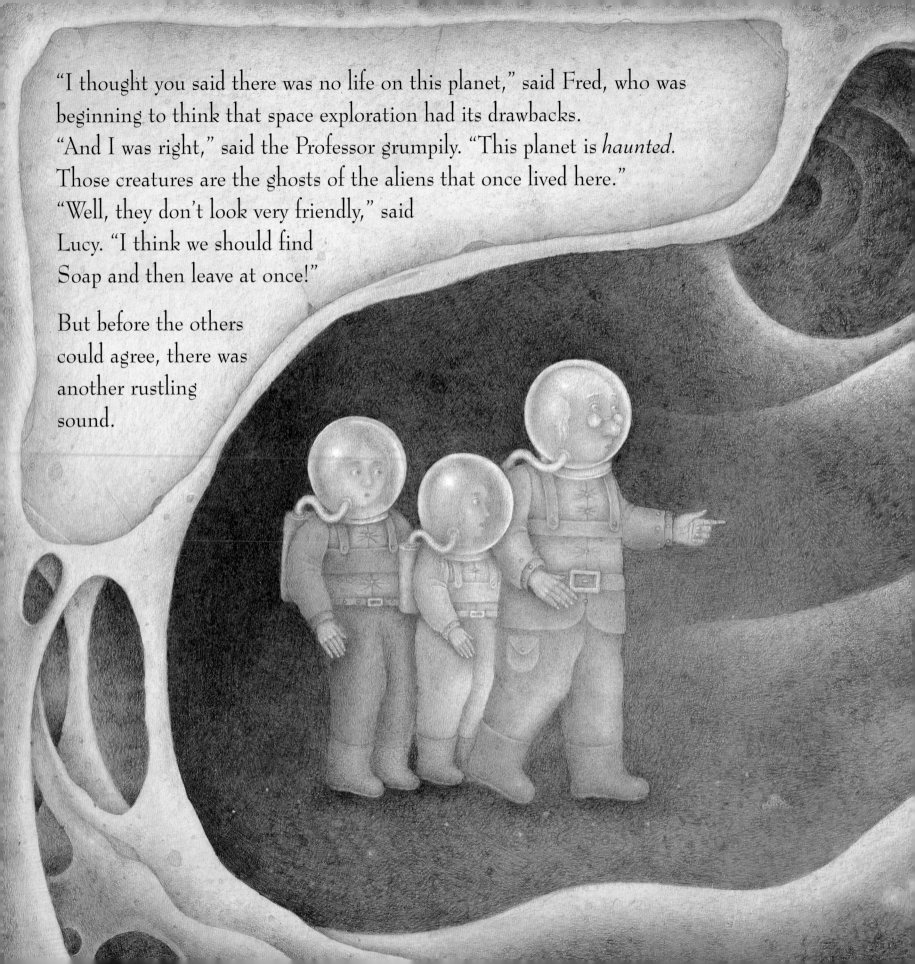

"I thought you said there was no life on this planet," said Fred, who was beginning to think that space exploration had its drawbacks.

"And I was right," said the Professor grumpily. "This planet is *haunted*. Those creatures are the ghosts of the aliens that once lived here."

"Well, they don't look very friendly," said Lucy. "I think we should find Soap and then leave at once!"

But before the others could agree, there was another rustling sound.

n front of them!

"T

crie

Ther

ghost

L

front of them!